Dear mouse friends,
Welcome to the world of

Geronimo Stilton

THE RODENT'S GAZETTE
EDITORIAL STAFF

Geronimo Stilton
A learned and brainy
mouse; editor of
The Rodent's Gazette

Thea Stilton
Geronimo's sister and
special correspondent at
The Rodent's Gazette

Trap Stilton
An awful joker;
Geronimo's cousin and
owner of the store
Cheap Junk for Less

Benjamin Stilton
A sweet and loving
nine-year-old mouse;
Geronimo's favorite
nephew

Geronimo Stilton

THE ENORMOUSE PEARL HEIST

Scholastic Inc.

ISBN 978-0-545-34103-5

Based on an original idea by Elisabetta Dami.

www.geronimostilton.com

Published by Scholastic Inc., 557 Broadway, New York, NY 10012. SCHOLASTIC and associated logos are trademarks and/or registered trademarks of Scholastic Inc.

Stilton is the name of a famous English cheese. It is a registered trademark of the Stilton Cheese Makers' Association. For more information, go to www.stiltoncheese.com.

Text by Geronimo Stilton
Original title *Il mistero della perla gigante*
Cover by Giuseppe Ferrario
Illustrations by Giuseppe Ferrario
Graphics by Michela Battaglin

Special thanks to Kathryn Cristaldi
Translated by Lidia Morson Tramontozzi
Interior design by Kay Petronio

12   17/0

Printed in the U.S.A.   40
First printing, October 2012

HISSSSS!

SIZZLING SWISS BITS! It was a blistering-hot summer. That day I had decided to skip the **HOT** subway ride and work from home. I was sweating at my desk, finishing up my latest **bestseller**, when suddenly . . .

Oops, how rude. I almost forgot to introduce myself. My name is Stilton, *Geronimo Stilton*. I am the editor of **The Rodent's Gazette**, the most popular paper on Mouse Island.

Argh!

Anyway, where was I? Oh, yes, I was tapping away at my computer when all of a sudden I heard a terrible hissing noise.

Hisssss! I nearly jumped out of my fur. It sounded like a den of snakes! I was about to climb up onto my desk when I heard a strange knocking sound:

KNOCK! KNOCK! KNOCK!

Before I could get to the door I heard a small explosion.

BANG!

Just then, black smoke started pouring out of my old air-conditioning unit. **Rats!** Immediately, it seemed like the room grew ten degrees **HOTTER**.

I tried calling all the appliance stores in New Mouse City to see if

I could get a new unit, but they were either out of stock or on vacation.

Sweat **trickled** down my fur. I was hotter than the award-winning entry at the New Mouse City *Great Balls of Fire Chili Cook-Off*!

To keep cool, I tried:

1. Eating tons of ice pops (but I got a stomachache).

2. Wrapping my head in frozen towels (but I got a headache).

3. Putting my paws in a pail of ice water (but the pail sprang a leak).

4. Taking a cold shower every thirty minutes (but that wasted too much time).

5. Turning on my giant fan (but my papers flew all over).

Finally, I couldn't take it anymore. "Drastic times call for drastic measures!" I said to myself. Then I filled the bathtub with **ice cubes**, grabbed my manuscript, and immersed myself in the **icy** water.

"Oh, it's so nice to be cool!" I squeaked happily.

I had just begun reading when the doorbell rang.

Oh, it's so nice to be cool!

DING-DONG! DING-DONG!

Holey cheese! I was so startled I almost dropped my manuscript into the water!

With a groan, I **CLIMBED** out of the bathtub, wrapped a towel around my waist, and went downstairs.

"This better be important," I mumbled, **flinging** the door open. A beautiful rodent stood before me.

Oops!

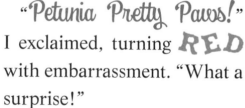

"*Petunia Pretty Paws!*" I exclaimed, turning **RED** with embarrassment. "What a surprise!"

A GIFT FOR ME?

"Hi, G!" she answered, bounding inside.

One thing you should know about Petunia: Besides being smart, beautiful, and kind, she has a **TON** of energy.

"How are you, Neputia — I mean Tepunia — I mean Petunia?" I babbled.

Oh, why do I always sound like such a fool around Petunia? It was bad enough that I was dressed in an old BATH TOWEL!

Hi, G!

After more humiliating **babbling**, I managed to explain to Petunia about my broken air conditioner. Then I told her to wait in the living room while I scampered off to get dressed.

I quickly threw on some clothes, poured two glasses of orange soda with **ice**, and returned to Petunia.

Just the sight of her made my heart go

In case you haven't guessed, **I HAVE A TOTAL CRUSH ON PETUNIA**. Too bad I'm too shy to tell her.

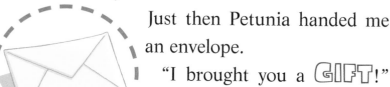

Just then Petunia handed me an envelope.

"I brought you a GIFT!" she said.

For me? I was so excited. Inside was a sheet of paper that said:

THIS CERTIFICATE
GOOD FOR:
Scuba-diving
lessons
on Shell Island!

I gulped. How could I tell Petunia I was **afraid** to scuba dive? I could barely swim! "Thanks, but—" I began.

But Petunia cut me off. "No buts, G. I'm going to Shell Island to **F** **I** **L** **M** a documentary, and I want you to come. It will be ƒʊn!" she insisted.

I was torn. On the one paw, I hate to fly, I

hate to swim in the ocean, and I hate to sleep in **strange** hotel beds. But on the other paw, how could I say no to the rodent of my dreams?

"Well, I guess . . ." I began.

"Great! It's settled," said Petunia. "We're bringing Benjamin and Bugsy Wugsy. *Aunt Sweetfur* is coming along to watch them while I work and you rest."

Another thing about Petunia: She's **super-organized**!

"When do we leave?" I asked.

"*Immediately!*" Petunia squeaked.

I'M READY!

Moldy mozzarella! It turned out Petunia wasn't exaggerating when she said we were leaving immediately. In fact, I had only **TEN MINUTES** to pack!

It's not easy to pack when you're rushed. I should know. When I packed in a rush once before, I forgot to bring lots of important things (like my **chamomile tea** and my Cheeseball the Clown night-light!).

After that happened, I promised myself I'd always be prepared. That's why I always keep **two** suitcases in my closet. The **RED** one is packed with everything I need for hot places. The **blue** one has everything I need for cold places.

So I grabbed the **RED** suitcase and raced back to Petunia.

"Okay, I'm ready!" I said triumphantly.

Petunia's jaw nearly **hit** the ground.

"How did you pack so *fast*?" she squeaked.

"It just takes practice," I answered with a grin.

I could tell Petunia was impressed.

My heart did a happy **flip-flop**.

I'm ready!

You're so fast!

A few minutes later we were in Petunia's **SUV**, headed for Aunt Sweetfur's to pick up her, Benjamin, and Bugsy Wugsy, who were all ready to go.

See what I mean about *Petunia* being organized?

When we arrived, Benjamin and Bugsy Wugsy hugged us. Actually, Bugsy nearly CHOKED me to death, but that's another story. . . .

Aunt Sweetfur kissed us hello. Then Uncle Grayfur clapped me on the back so **hard** I felt like I might never walk again. For a retired sea captain, that old rodent sure is **STRONG**!

"I'd give my whiskers to come with you!" Uncle

Grayfur bellowed. "But I've got an important conference at the **Old Captain's Lodge**, and I can't miss it. Have a nice trip—just watch out for **SHARKS**!"

Everybody laughed. Except for me. I chewed my pawnails. **OUCH!** Did I mention how much I hate swimming in the ocean?

After we climbed into the car, Aunt Sweetfur blew a **KISS** to Uncle Grayfur, and we left.

I was trying to relax when Bugsy began to sing, "**I know a song that drives everybody crazy!**" **OVER** and **OVER**.

This was going to be a **long** trip!

IS THIS YOURS?

By the time we got to the airport, my head was **pounding**. But, since I am a true **gentlemouse**, I still offered to carry all the suitcases. Unfortunately, the rolling carts were all taken, so I had to carry everything **by paw**. My back was killing me!

But that was only the beginning. . . .

We were waiting for our suitcases to go through the **security** scanner, when the last **Whew!** bag on the conveyor belt set off the alarm. Beep! Beep! I stared in **horror** at the suitcase. It was mine!

"Is this yours?" a uniformed agent asked.

When I said yes, he asked me to open it. I'll admit, I was a little embarrassed to have security pawing through my personal belongings. What if he saw my **night-light**? Or my Swiss cheese **underwear**? Still, I had no choice.

So I lifted the lid and discovered . . . ten **bulky** sweaters, a *wool* hat, waterproof **GLOVES**, hiking **BOOTS**, and an **ice** pickax for glaciers!

Rat-munching rattlesnakes!

I had somehow switched the contents of my cold-weather suitcase with the contents of my hot-weather suitcase!

"You can't carry a sharp **ice** pickax on an airplane! It's dangerous!" the agent scolded. "Where are you going?"

I coughed. "Ahem . . . I'm going to . . . Shell Island, where I'm going to learn . . ." I was so EMBARRASSED I didn't want to tell him what I was doing, but knew I should. ". . . scuba diving," I mumbled, turning **beet red**.

The agent looked at me sternly. "Well, then you won't need the pickax!" he said, and took it away.

AN ALARMING PILOT

"What am I going to do with these clothes?" I wailed when I got the suitcase back.

"Don't worry, G!" Petunia consoled me. "It was a simple mix-up. And this means that when we get to the island, we're going **shopping**!"

I sighed. Oh, how I hate **shopping**!

"Come on, *let's move it* — our plane's about to leave!" Petunia said.

If I knew what was waiting for me on the plane, I would have turned around and gone to the mountains! There were no regular flights to Shell Island, so the TV station Petunia was working for had organized a private flight.

The problem, however, was not the plane,

but the pilot! He looked like an aviator from the last century with his leather helmet and pair of goggles covered with dust. He also had a very loud voice.

"WELCOME ABOARD!" he shouted as soon as we boarded. "MY NAME IS FLASH PIROUETTE, AND I AM CAPTAIN OF THIS AIRCRAFT. BUCKLE YOUR SEAT BELTS AND BRING YOUR SEAT TO AN UPRIGHT POSITION! WE ARE ABOUT TO TAKE OFF!"

FLASH PIROUETTE

"He knows what he's doing, right?" I asked Petunia.

"He sure does!" she answered with a *smile*. She continued excitedly, "He's so good, he's won the **MOUSE ISLAND**

STUNT FLYING CHAMPIONSHIP twice!"

As if he had heard her, Flash began ZiGZAGGiNG between the clouds, *up* and down and up and down.

YiKES! Even if I wasn't such a scaredy-mouse, I think that might have been too much for me!

Finally, we cleared the clouds and the airplane settled into a normal flight path. After an hour, we came in sight of Shell Island.

"There it is!" exclaimed Petunia, pointing to a tiny emerald-green spot shining in the middle of the **dark-blue** South Mousific Ocean. It didn't look inhabited other than one small settlement.

"I can't see the RUNWAY for the plane," I said worriedly.

"Of course you can't! There isn't any!"

"Wh-what do you mean there's no runway? How are we going to **land**?"

"We'll land in the *WATER* and we'll get to shore with the airplane's life raft!" Petunia explained.

"**WHAAAAAAAAAAAAT? HEEEEEEEELP!**" I yelled, terrified.

Suddenly, the plane veered to the side and headed straight toward the ocean at full speed.

YIKES! I wanted to live!

Luckily, despite what I predicted, Flash landed the plane *gently* and smoothly. We got to shore in no time at all.

A strange rodent greeted us on the beach.

"Welcome to Shell Island, Mr. Stilton! We've been waiting for you!"

THE PROVOLONE FAMILY

"My name is **PINCH PROVOLONE**, and I am the manager of the island's only hotel," the rodent continued.

"Nice to meet you," I replied.

"Please let my children Simon and Sinbad help you with your luggage," he said.

PINCH PROVOLONE

Two **muscular** rodents began unloading our luggage while Pinch greeted Petunia and the others.

Of course, Pinch had recognized Petunia. Did I mention that she is a popular **TV**

REPORTER famouse for saving animals and the environment?

I was staring admiringly at Petunia when all of a sudden a voice yelled, "**Watch out!**"

I saw a female rodent waving her paws at me.

Then everything went **BLACK**.

I had been accidentally **SMACKED** in the head with a suitcase!

When I came to, the hotel manager said,

"By the way, that was my daughter, Serena. She'll show you to your room."

When we reached my room, Petunia got me a bag of **ice** for the lump that was forming on my head. Aunt Sweetfur sat by me and held my paw. "Smell this, deary," she said, shoving a little **purple** bottle under my nose. "It's perfumed cheese, ideal for headaches."

I closed my eyes. Aunt Sweetfur was right. I felt a lot better. I thought about Pinch Provolone and his three children, **SIMON**, **SINBAD**, and Serena. There was something about them that made them all look the **same**. What was it?

CLUE no. 1

WHAT ARE ALL THE PROVOLONE CHILDREN WEARING THAT IS THE SAME?

Gold earrings!

STAY STILL!

The next morning, I was having a fabumouse dream in which Petunia and I were riding the **WAVES** on the back of a dolphin. But it was interrupted by someone knocking at my door.

"Who is it?" I mumbled.

It was Petunia.

"Did you forget, G? We have to go **shopping**!" she squeaked.

Thundering cattails! I knew I couldn't wear my winter boots on the beach, but I still hate **shopping**!

Before I knew it, Petunia was **DRAGGING** me all over the place. We scurried from store to store like two mice in a rat race. When we left I was wearing:

1. an orange flowered shirt
2. **pea-green** Bermuda shorts
3. bright **purple** sandals
4. a **Multicolored** cap.

Ugh!

I felt like a color-blind tourist.

"You look great, G!" exclaimed Petunia. Then she said good-bye and went off to begin filming her **DOCUMENTARY** on the island.

Benjamin tried not to laugh when he saw me, but Bugsy Wugsy collapsed in a fit of giggles.

Aunt Sweetfur **SHOOED** them away.

"You look wonderful! All you need is a touch of lilac," she said as she, wrapped a purple scarf around my neck.

How **embarrassing**! But what could I do? I couldn't insult my *sweet* aunt. So, dressed in that outfit, I left for my first scuba-diving lesson.

When I reached the pier, my instructor was already waiting for me aboard a little MOTORIZED dinghy.

Strange. He looked just like Simon, one of Pinch Provolone's sons.

"Surprised, Mr. Stilton?" he asked. "I help my dad in the hotel, and I'm also a **diving** instructor. But don't worry — I've only lost **one** of my students so far. And it wasn't my fault. It was the shark's."

The shark's fault? My whiskers twitched nervously. Oh, how I wished I were home!

Before I knew it, Simon was helping me

into my scuba suit. It was exhausting getting into all that rubber. My fur felt like it was being ripped off, and I was sweating like crazy.

Then, when Simon tried to help me into the boat, I tripped and ended up in the water!

SPLASH!

After he fished me out and deposited me back in the dinghy, I waved a miserable good-bye to Aunt Sweetfur, Benjamin, and Bugsy Wugsy.

Who knew if I'd ever see them again?

We left the pier and headed off.

Once we hit the open SEA, Simon helped me put on my fins, mask, and tank.

"Now sit there on the edge of the dinghy,

and whatever you do, **DON'T MOVE**!" he instructed.

I did my best to stay still, but the boat was **rocking** back and forth, and the weight of the tank made me feel completely **UNBALANCED**.

Stay still! Stay still! I told myself. But it didn't work.

A minute later, I fell **BACKWARD** into the

SPLASH!

water . . . again! How humiliating! And **SCARY**! And *I saw something TERRIFYING* down there before Simon fished me out.

"Why didn't you stay still, Mr. Stilton?" he asked, looking slightly annoyed.

"I tried, but the boat was rocking too much, and the tank is so **heavy**, and — " I mumbled.

Simon rolled his eyes. "Okay, okay," he said, cutting me off. "But you have to listen, or you'll never get to do any diving."

To be honest, I wasn't sure I ever wanted to get back into the water after what I'd seen.

"Something down there tried to EAT me!" I told Simon. "It looked like a gigantic **blue** fish with enormouse teeth!"

"A giant **blue** fish with big teeth?" Simon asked with a smirk.

"Not just **big** teeth," I corrected him. "They were huge, like **DAGGERS**!"

Simon snorted. It was clear he didn't believe me.

CODFISH ICE CREAM

That evening at dinner, we all took turns talking about our day. Benjamin and Bugsy Wugsy had gone swimming and made a **s a n d** sculpture. Aunt Sweetfur had collected little lilac-colored seashells  to make a pretty necklace. And Petunia had filmed a lot of the island and was already planning what she would shoot the next day.

I was hoping no one would notice I hadn't said anything when Benjamin said, "How about you, Uncle G? How was your first diving lesson?"

"Ahem, well, it was . . . er . . . pretty, um,

good. . . ." I mumbled. What could I say? It was a total disaster. I was a complete **KLUTZ**. I had to be rescued **twice**!

Just then Pinch Provolone appeared with a **huge** platter of fish for the table.

"Don't be shy, Mr. Stilton!" he chuckled. "Tell your friends about the **big blue** fish that almost ate you alive!"

I turned **RED**. I guess word traveled fast on the island.

"You saw a **big blue** fish and you didn't tell us?" Petunia squeaked. "Tomorrow I'm coming with you. I've got to **FILM** it!"

Immediately, I felt better. At least someone believed me!

I was so happy that *Petunia* was going to come diving with me, I couldn't stop smiling.

Dreamily, I shoved a forkful of squid covered in **RED** sauce into my mouth. Big mistake! It was SPICY!

"FIIIIIIIIIIIIIIIIIIIIIIIIRE!" I shouted. "I'm BUUUURNIIIIIIIING!"

Pinch grabbed a bucket of **ice water** and poured it over me.

"Oops!" he said when he realized his mistake.

Ugh!

All better?

Water **dripped** down my fur, forming a puddle around me. I wrung out my tail, feeling like a drowned rat.

To make it up to me, Pinch insisted I try their special dessert: codfish ice cream.

Note to self: Ice cream + Fish = Yuck!

I went to bed totally nauseous, and dreamed I was being chased by a giant mouse-eating blue fish!

A GIANT OYSTER!

The following morning Aunt Sweetfur woke me up at six fifteen.

"I have to talk to you, dear," she whispered **MYSTERIOUSLY**.

I was so tired, I felt like I had been in the ring with **MUHAMMAD SQUEAKLI**, the heavyweight boxing legend. Oh, why was Aunt Sweetfur waking me up at such an unmousely hour?

"I was so intrigued by your story about the gigantic **blue** fish, I called your uncle Grayfur," she explained. "He told me there's only one creature living in the South Mousific Ocean with those characteristics. He also said that it's not a fish — it's a **huge**

oyster. It's a special species that is referred to as **The Eye of the Ocean**. They're usually as large as a fist, but, in extremely rare cases, they can become **enormouse** — and that's when they are very valuable."

"Why?" I asked, becoming more curious.

"I don't know. The line went dead and I couldn't ask him. Oh, well, go back to sleep,

It's a giant oyster!

dearest nephew. *Sweet dreams!*"

After Aunt Sweetfur left, I couldn't fall asleep. I kept thinking about the **giant oyster**. Then just as I was starting to *drift off*, Petunia came into my room fully dressed.

"So, are we going? The SUN is about to rise!" she squeaked cheerfully. "The Provolone brothers said I have a better chance of spotting the blue fish if we get there at the crack of dawn. I'll meet you at the pier, G!"

Reluctantly, I left my w a R M bed, got dressed, and headed for the pier. Simon, Sinbad, and Petunia were waiting for me.

Once again, I struggled to get into my wetsuit. What a workout! By the time I put on my suit, mask, fins, and the heavy oxygen tank, I was ready for a nap!

Instead, we took off for **deep waters**. When we arrived, Simon said, "To be safe, I will be diving with you, Mr. Stilton."

Then he buckled a **weighted** belt around my waist.

"This is a ballast," Simon explained. "It's used to help you get to the **bottom**."

I gulped. But what if I wanted to get to the **top**? I was about to ask Simon when suddenly he yelled, "*GO!*"

Then he threw me into the water!

A DROWNED RAT?

The good thing was, I was so surprised that I didn't have time to **SCREAM** and embarrass myself in front of Petunia. The bad thing was, I was so **surprised** that I held my breath! Immediately, I began to feel *DIZZY*.

Then I felt someone grab my paw. It was *Petunia*, signaling me to breathe. So much for not embarrassing myself! I followed her advice and realized I didn't need to hold my breath — I had on an oxygen tank.

At that moment, Simon motioned for us to follow him.

But I couldn't. The ballast was dragging me **straight to the bottom!**

I tried to move my fins like everyone else, but instead of going forward, I found myself **spinning** over and over. I looked like I was doing some kind of spastic *underwater* ballet!

Luckily, Simon noticed and swam over to help me. Meanwhile, Petunia turned on the *underwater* video camera. I timidly **FLIPPED** my fins and was happy to see I was moving in the right direction.

For a while, I swam behind Petunia and Simon, feeling pretty confident. Maybe this scuba-diving thing wasn't so hard after all. Maybe it could even be **fun**. Maybe . . .

A second later, one of the flippers *slipped* from my paw and I was left **kicking** sideways like a fish with one fin. Oh, **why** did these things always happen to me?

The ballast started **DRAGGING** me deeper and deeper toward the bottom. I wanted to **SCREAM** but I couldn't, and no one noticed me.

Simon was leading the way. And Petunia was so intent on **FILMING** that nothing would have distracted her.

Headlines flashed before my eyes:

GLUB...
GLUB...

Publisher's Deadly Dive! Geronimo Stilton: The Story of a Drowned Rat!

The water was becoming **dark** and murky. It was so **spooky**. Could things get any worse?

Then they did. Suddenly, I noticed a sparkling light below me. I looked down and saw the gigantic **blue** fish!

Its mouth was wide open, and I was **TUMBLING** right into it!

AAAAAAAAAAAAAAAAAAAAAAAAAAAAAAAAAAAAAAAAAAAA

THE EYE OF THE OCEAN

Desperately, I began fumbling with the weight belt, trying to unbuckle it, but my paws were trembling so much I was getting nowhere. I sank **DEEPER** and **DEEPER**.

Thundering cattails! The enormouse jaws of the **blue** fish were closing in on me! I was about to become a mouthful of furry fish food!

I looked up for the last time and I thought I could see the **light** from Petunia's camera coming toward me. *Good-bye, sweet Petunia!* I **sobbed** to myself. *Good-bye, family! Good-bye, world!*

But when I looked down again, I saw the most amazing sight. It was an **enoRmouse**

blue **oyster**, and its shell was completely open. In its center sat a huge, glowing pearl.

I couldn't believe my eyes! Uncle Grayfur was right! I hadn't seen a gigantic blue fish — I had discovered the famous giant oyster, also known as **The Eye of the Ocean**!

Unfortunately, as soon as I hit bottom, I kicked up a CLOUD of sand, and the shell snapped itself shut as if it wanted to protect its treasure.

A minute later, Simon also arrived. Simon tried to open the blue pod with his bare paws, but the oyster's shell was completely sealed.

He tried to force it with a rock, but still it wouldn't open.

I was glad Petunia *motioned* for

him to stop. The oyster was so *beautiful*. It would be awful if he ruined it.

Finally, Simon removed my **weighted** belt and signaled for us to go up. I couldn't wait to reach the boat.

A VERY RICH MOUSE!

As soon as we got out of the water, Simon told Sinbad all about the **treasure** I had discovered.

"I think it's the biggest example of The Eye of the Ocean that has ever been found," he said.

Then for some reason, the two of them exchanged an odd look.

How **STRANGE**!

Meanwhile, Petunia was beaming. "I'm so glad I was able to **F** **I** **L** **M** the shell before it closed! I can air this piece during my broadcast on the South Mousific Ocean!" she squeaked.

"And I can write up an article for *The Rodent's Gazette* today, and email it to the office," I added. "Tomorrow the amazing discovery of **The Eye of the Ocean** will be plastered all over the FRONT PAGE!"

Suddenly, my near-**drowning** experience seemed like it had been a lifetime ago. I was so excited about the **oyster**, I hardly noticed Simon and Sinbad shooting me **strange** looks. Maybe they were staring at my fur. It was sticking up all over the place after our dive.

Later at dinner, Pinch Provolone explained that since I had found the sea pearl, tradition ruled that it belonged to me. "You are a very **RICH** mouse, Mr. Stilton!" he declared.

Then he promised that his whole family would be more than happy to help me retrieve the **enoRmoUSe** oyster from the bottom of the sea.

Aunt Sweetfur, Benjamin, and Bugsy Wugsy wanted to hear all about how I found the **oyster**, so I told them.

"I wonder how much that pearl is worth!" Bugsy thought aloud when I had finished.

"It's priceless!" Benjamin answered.

Aunt Sweetfur nodded. "It seems a shame to take something so *precious* from the ocean. Maybe it is best to **LEAVE** it where it is. What do you think, Geronimo? After all, it is your decision."

I scratched my head. On the one paw, it would be an amazing treasure to own. But on the other paw, I agreed with Aunt Sweetfur. The pearl belonged to the OCEAN. I knew I had to do the right thing.

Finally, I said, "I will publish my find in the paper, and Petunia will air her piece on TV, but we will leave the **oyster** in its

natural home: the **ocean**."

Petunia looked at me with **tears** in her eyes.

"Oh, G, you're such a **gentlemouse**," she said with a sigh.

I was so busy staring into Petunia's eyes, I didn't notice Simon, Sinbad, and Serena

Yes, a gentlemouse!

scamper out of the room. But Benjamin and Bugsy did, and they were worried.

"Uncle Geronimo, where is your **laptop**?" Benjamin squeaked.

"And where is your video **CAMERA**, Aunt Petunia?" Bugsy added.

A bad feeling *washed* over me. . . .

CLUE Nº. 2 ◄-------

WHAT ARE BENJAMIN AND BUGSY WORRIED ABOUT?

That someone will steal the camera and computer.

STOLEN?

I ran to my room to check on my **LƎPTOP** while Petunia checked her room for her video camera. Moldy mozzarella! They were both **MISSING**!

Now I couldn't send my article to *The Rodent's Gazette,* and Petunia couldn't air the film she had taken of **The Eye of the Ocean**. I was in **SHOCK**! Was someone out to **steal** the giant oyster and its giant pearl before we spread the news of its discovery?

But who?

We headed down to the lobby to talk to the manager.

"**Stolen?**" Pinch said when he heard our news. "How strange. Nothing like this

has ever happened in my hotel. Who could it have been?"

Petunia crossed her paws. "Maybe you could tell us where your **children** ran off to after dinner," she said.

But just then Simon, Sinbad, and Serena arrived carrying a large **cheesecake** platter. "We were just getting dessert. Want some?" Serena squeaked.

I was going to ask why it took **three** mice to carry **one** platter, but I was too busy **drooling**. Did I mention I love **cheesecake**?

"We will keep our eyes peeled for the missing items," Pinch assured me as I nibbled **one tiny** piece of cheesecake. Well, okay, maybe it was more like **four giant** pieces of cheesecake, but who's counting?

Just then Aunt Sweetfur appeared. "I hope

I called!

you don't mind, Geronimo," she said, "but I called *The Rodent's Gazette* and told them about **The Eye of the Ocean**. I said you would contact them with the details. Is that okay?"

"**Perfect!**" I beamed. "And tomorrow Petunia and I can go back and record more footage."

For some reason, the **PROVOLONE FAMILY** looked less than excited.

But there was no time to worry about them now. I had to **call** the paper, and maybe take **one** more piece of cheesecake . . . I couldn't resist!

Finally, I called *The Rodent's Gazette*. When I was done squeaking, I sat down on my bed and screamed.

"OUCH!"

A splinter was stuck in my paw! Aunt Sweetfur gently removed it and held it up.

It wasn't a splinter. It was a **gold** earring! Whose could it be?

That night I couldn't get to sleep. Partly because I couldn't stop thinking about the

earring. And partly because I had a terrible Stomachache. Oh, why had I eaten all that cheesecake?!

clue nº. 3

DO YOU KNOW WHO LOST A GOLD EARRING?

Serena Provolone! Compare the pictures on pages 24 and 53.

PROFESSOR GIL FISHYWHISKERS

The following morning **The Rodent's Gazette** sold out all across New Mouse City.

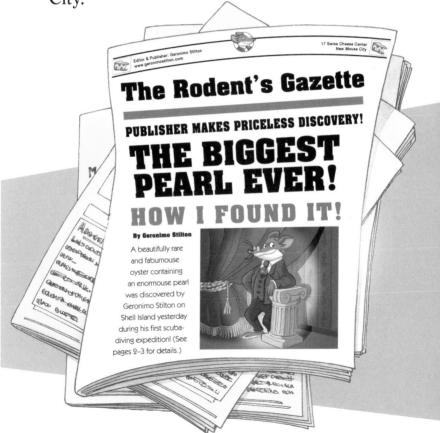

Editor & Publisher: Geronimo Stilton
www.geronimostilton.com

17 Swiss Cheese Center
New Mouse City

The Rodent's Gazette

PUBLISHER MAKES PRICELESS DISCOVERY!

THE BIGGEST PEARL EVER!

HOW I FOUND IT!

By Geronimo Stilton

A beautifully rare and fabumouse oyster containing an enormouse pearl was discovered by Geronimo Stilton on Shell Island yesterday during his first scuba-diving expedition! (See pages 2–3 for details.)

In just a few hours, the news of my **discovery** had spread all over the island.

Then a **strange** thing happened. Pinch Provolone knocked at my door. "We found your **COMPUTER**, Mr. Stilton," he said. "The housekeeper found it in the hallway along with Petunia's video camera."

He was about to leave when I stopped him. "Wait!" I said, handing him the **gold** earring I had found in my room. "Whoever took my computer must have lost this."

Pinch turned **RED**, grabbed the earring, and disappeared.

It was then that I remembered who wore **gold** earrings — the Provolone children!

Just then my cell phone began *ringing* like crazy. So much for the quick ratnap I was hoping to catch . . .

Here's who called me on the phone:

Hello?

1. **SALLY RATMOUSEN**, who was so jealous she could hardly squeak;

2. **Grandfather William Shortpaws**, who was so happy he could hardly squeak;

3. **Mayor Frederick Fuzzypaws**, who wanted to exhibit the shell at the New Mouse City Mouseum of Natural History;

4. Twenty-five collectors who wanted to buy the pearl;

5. Twenty-five jewelers who wanted to buy the pearl;

And many others!

By the time I hung up, I was *exhausted*. I went to find my friends.

"I don't know what to do," I squeaked worriedly. "Everyone wants to get their paws on the pearl!"

I chewed on my whiskers, feeling helpless. How could I make sure that **The Eye of the Ocean** was safe? Anyone could *steal* it from the ocean. The more I thought about it, the more hopeless I felt. Before long I was sobbing like a newborn mouselet. How humiliating!

Petunia interrupted my crying jag. "Cheer up, G," she said. "I have a plan!"

Then she told me that she had called Uncle Grayfur, and he had given her the number of the director of the New Mouse City Aquarium. His name was **Professor Gil Fishywhiskers**.

"He's an old friend of your uncle's. He'll help us!" Petunia insisted.

Soon I was on the phone with **Professor Fishywhiskers**. The minute I introduced myself, he began squeaking so **FAST** I wondered how he was able to breathe. I couldn't get a word in edgewise!

Apparently, he, too, had read the paper, and was thrilled by my discovery.

Don't move!

"**Don't move** from where you are!" he shouted excitedly. "I'll be on Shell Island sometime in the morning with the proper gear. That oyster needs to be removed VERY CAREFULLY. It's an extremely rare specimen!"

I hung up the **phone** feeling a whole lot better. Professor Fishywhiskers to the rescue!

But just then I had a thought that made me *SHUDDER*.

What if the Provolone siblings had already taken the **oyster** last night?

Lucky for me, Petunia read my mind.

"Don't worry about the Provolones, G. I didn't want them to **steal** the oyster, so yesterday I took the **plug** from their boat!" she giggled, holding up the plug.

Hee hee hee!

PLUG FOR THE DINGHY

Grrr . . .

Who took it?

IT'S AN INVASION!

Even though we had the plug from the Provolones' boat, we decided it would be a good idea to keep an eye on them anyway.

Aunt Sweetfur offered to watch the beach with Benjamin and Bugsy Wugsy while Petunia and I hung around the hotel.

But first we had to eat breakfast. I was starving! I had just ordered the Shell Island Happy Morning Special — a three-cheese omelette, cheddar homefries, a mozzarella milkshake, and a fruit bowl — when we heard a LOUD noise coming from the docks.

Outside we saw dozens of boats sailing into the port. Reporters, collectors, and other curious rodents were swarming the island, hoping to sneak a PEEK at

Mr. Stilton!

The Eye of the Ocean! Pinch Provolone was **HYSTERICAL**. "It's an invasion! Do something, Mr. Stilton!" he squeaked.

I had to admit, it was a little SCARY to see all these rodents clambering up the beach, squeaking at the top of their lungs. Still, I tried to remain calm.

"It's okay," I told Pinch. "In a few hours, a team from the New Mouse City Aquarium will be here to remove the **oyster**, and everything will be back to NORMAL."

Pinch nodded, but he didn't look happy. He ran off and began CHATTERING up a storm with Simon.

Fortunately, Professor Fishywhiskers was a mouse of his word. It wasn't long before he arrived in a strange-looking craft that read

New Mouse City Aquarium Laboratory Ship on its side.

I shook paws with the professor and we all boarded the ship.

As soon as we got on board, Simon ran over to the ship's captain, and the two began whispering. It seemed Simon and **Captain B. Crooked Paw** (also known as Old Crook, Cap Paw, and The Crookinator) knew each other well.

Ahoy there, Geronimo!

New Mouse City Aquarium Laboratory Ship

How **strange**!

But there was no time to think about it. Before long, we reached the area where we first found the oyster. A scuba diver J**U**M**P**ED into the water. I held my breath. I was a **wreck**.

What if something had *happened* to the oyster?

Captain B. Crooked Paw

SPECTACULAR!

I stared into the water, feeling faint. If the oyster was missing, everyone would think I was a **lying cheesebrain**!

I was so worried I hardly noticed the **boats** around our ship filled with reporters, collectors, and other sightseers.

Finally, the diver resurfaced. He had **found** the oyster! He put it in a safety net, and Captain Crooked Paw used a crane to hoist it up.

As soon as **The Eye of the Ocean** emerged from the sea, the crowd cheered. It was **spectacular**!

Video cameras rolled and cameras flashed again and again as everyone gawked at the incredible, **enormouse** oyster.

"Slowly, Captain! **BE CAREFUL!**" Professor Fishywhiskers warned.

The captain lowered the oyster through a large trapdoor that led to the holding tank. We raced **DOWN** the stairs after it as Petunia filmed the entire thing. Then the professor began examining the shell, taking its **WEIGHT** and measurements, and photographing it from every angle.

Finally, the oyster was X-rayed, revealing the **enormouse** pearl hidden inside.

"It's absolutely **fabumouse**!" exclaimed the professor as soon as he saw the X-ray.

"Now what are we going to do?" I asked the professor. I was feeling very responsible for the oyster and was still a little **nervous** that someone might damage it.

"Don't worry. We'll immerse the oyster in a specially made tank filled with **seawater**.

Then we'll place the tank into a **wooden** crate cushioned with packing material, and transport it home," he explained. "We've got a beautiful new tank at the aquarium ready to hold it. Rodents will come from all over the world to admire this RARE find."

I sighed with relief. I was so glad the professor had arrived and taken control of

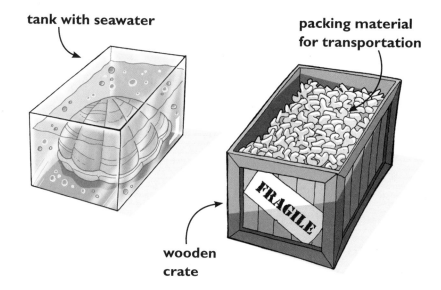

tank with seawater

packing material for transportation

wooden crate

FRAGILE

the situation. Being **responsible** for such a priceless treasure was making my whiskers twitch.

Now everyone watched as the giant oyster was placed in the wooden crate and SEALED shut. Then Simon asked a question I hadn't even thought about.

"Once the closed shell is settled in your aquarium, Professor, how will anyone be able to see the **enormouse** pearl inside?" he said.

The professor nodded knowingly. "Young mouse, I'm happy to inform you that I know the SECRET to opening the shell without damaging it in any way. Of course, I can't tell you HOW I do it, for security reasons — you understand. But if you come to the New Mouse City Aquarium, I guarantee you will see the **enormouse** pearl in all its glory!" he squeaked excitedly.

Simon nodded, then exchanged a **look** with the captain.

How **strange** . . .

A Bad Feeling

By the time the oyster was packed up safe and sound, it was *dusk*. The professor wanted to leave immediately, but Captain Crooked Paw refused to sail.

"We'll spend the **NIGHT** at the dock, then leave first thing in the morning," he insisted.

Later at dinner, Professor Fishywhiskers stroked his beard **nervously**. "I'm not sure why, but I have a **bad** feeling," he confessed. "I think it would be a good idea if we all keep an **eye** on the oyster tonight."

Petunia and I volunteered to stay on the boat and guard the **oyster** while Aunt Sweetfur stayed with Benjamin and Bugsy Wugsy in the hotel.

After dinner, we went back to the laboratory ship to spend the night. I have to admit, I wasn't crazy about the idea of **SLEEPING** on a boat. Did I mention that I get **seasick**?

Oh, well. At least the boat was staying at the dock. I was just thinking that maybe I shouldn't have eaten that second loaded cheddarburger, when the professor waved us into his cabin.

"I'm worried!" he whispered. "The oyster is in DANGER, and I may be as well. If something happens to me, I want you to know how to open **The Eye of the Ocean** without harming it."

I'm worried!

"Don't be silly, Professor," Petunia reassured him.

But the professor insisted. He whispered

the **SECRET** in our ears. Petunia and I looked at each other, surprised.

"Now that I told you, I feel better," said the professor. "Go and take your watch **GUARDING** the oyster. We'll say good-bye tomorrow morning."

Petunia and I settled ourselves on the ship's deck wrapped in **WOOLEN** blankets. Above us, the sky was filled with stars.

What a starry sky!

For a while, I forgot about the oyster. It was a beautiful night, and I was with the mouse of my DREAMS! Too bad I was tired. Before long, I was snoring away. When I woke up at dawn, I was drooling. How embarrassing!

Even worse — when I went to check on the oyster, I discovered the professor had disappeared!

clue nº. 4

CAN YOU GUESS WHAT HAPPENED TO THE PROFESSOR?

He was mousenapped!

OPEN THAT CRATE!

We looked for the **PROFESSOR** everywhere. Aunt Sweetfur, Benjamin, Bugsy Wugsy, and even some of the PROVOLONE FAMILY helped us search. But there was no trace of him. He had VANISHED!

Where had he gone? My mind raced.

Back at the pier, we saw a helicopter **circling** the beach. Simon was showing it where to land.

Meanwhile, on the ship, Captain Crooked Paw was using the crane to **LiFT** the crate containing the oyster *up* into the air.

"**Stop!**" I cried. "What's going on?"

Captain Crooked Paw stared down at me

with **STEELY** eyes. "Mr. Stilton, I am only protecting the oyster," he announced. "It's not safe on this ship now that the professor has **disappeared**, so I called the aquarium's head office. They sent us a helicopter to transport the oyster."

The captain was right. The ship was not safe anymore. What if the **oyster** went **MISSING**, just like the professor? Still, something was **BOTHERING** me.

"Okay," I agreed. "But before you leave, I want to make sure the **oyster** is still in its place."

"That means we'll have to open the crate. It will take **TOO LONG**, right, Captain?" Simon objected.

Suddenly, as I stared at Simon and the crate, I realized what was **BOTHERING** me.

"Captain, I insist you OPEN that crate now!" I demanded.

"All right, all right," the captain grumbled. "Don't get your whiskers in a **twist**."

clue nº. 5 ← - - - - - - - ¬

DO YOU SEE WHAT GERONIMO NOTICED ABOUT THE CRATE AND SIMON?

The word *fragile* is spelled wrong, and Simon has red paint on his paws.

EVERYTHING'S THE SAME

Reluctantly, the captain lifted the **lid** off the crate and everyone peeked inside. At first, I was relieved. The oyster was still there, immersed in the **water**. But then I noticed something **strange**.

"That's odd. It doesn't seem like the same **oyster**. . . ." I murmured.

The captain scoffed, "Of course it's the same one." He reached for the lid, struggling to replace it.

"It's exactly the same," added Simon, who was **sweating** like a sprinkler.

"I think it looks fine, G," said Petunia, *winking* at me.

"Everything's the same," Aunt Sweetfur

agreed, *winking* at me as well.

What was with all the winking? Was my FUR a mess? Did I have a piece of CHEESE stuck between my teeth?

I looked at Benjamin. "The oyster looks perfect, Uncle Geronimo," he announced, shooting me a look.

Bugsy Wugsy nodded, grabbing my paw and squeezing it **hard**. Youch! I chewed my whiskers to keep from squeaking.

What was everyone trying to TELL me?

I was still trying to figure it out when the captain interrupted my thoughts. "See, there's NO problem!" he declared.

A minute later, he signaled for the helicopter to remove the crate. Then the captain and Simon **disappeared** into the ship.

"Do you think it will get there **safely**?" I asked.

"It doesn't matter, G," Petunia said. "Because the **real** oyster is not in that crate! It's a **fake**! We all realized, but we didn't want the captain or any of the Provolones to know we are onto them. That's what we were trying to tell you."

I nodded SLOWLY. So that's why everyone was winking at me!

Still, I was confused. "But how can you be so sure it's a **fake**?" I asked.

Benjamin smiled. "It was simple, Uncle Geronimo. We just **studied** the shell," he explained.

CLUE №. 6

DO YOU KNOW WHY EVERYONE THINKS THE OYSTER IS FAKE?

Compare the picture on page 87 with the picture on page 73. The real oyster's shell has five ribs. The fake one has only four.

PETUNIA'S NOTE

Petunia explained to me that the real oyster's shell has FIVE ribs on it, while the fake one has only **four**. Now I knew why something seemed different about the shell. The captain and the Provolones were out to **trick** us. They were out to **steal** the oyster!

All of a sudden I felt sick. If the REAL oyster wasn't on its way to New Mouse City, then where was it? Was it still on the island? And where was Professor Fishywhiskers?

Back at the hotel, my mind raced. This trip was turning into a total NIGHTMARE. What else could go wrong?

I was so worried about everything, I couldn't think straight. I chewed my pawnails, and my tail wouldn't stop **twitching**.

To calm my **nerves**, I tried doing a few relaxing yoga moves I had learned from my cousin Serenity Stilton. They didn't work. Instead, I ended up twisting myself up like a pretzel. **Ugh!**

Next I tried drinking a **soothing** cup of chamomile tea. But it was too HOT, and I burned my tongue. Ouch!

Then I decided to take a nice warm bath. Too bad I accidentally poured **suntan lotion** into the tub instead of bubble bath. **YUCK!**

Finally, I gave up and headed off to dinner. Aunt Sweetfur, Benjamin, and Bugsy Wugsy were all waiting for me.

But where was Petunia?

No one had seen her.

We decided to check her room. When we got there, I knocked, but there was no answer.

The door wasn't **LOCKED**, so we went in. The room was empty. Then, I spotted a SMALL note on the dresser. It was addressed **"To Geronimo**."

I opened it with **trembling** paws. It read:

There's a big cave on the west side of the beach. I might have found the oyster . . . and something else as well. I'll wait for you there. Hurry!

Petunia

P.S. Bring Aunt Sweetfur's flute.

THE CAVE

My fur stood on **END**, but there was no time to take another crack at those *relaxing* yoga moves now. We had to find Petunia!

Aunt Sweetfur grabbed the *flute* and we all snuck off into the night.

Luckily, Benjamin had brought along a **flashlight**, which we used to find our

Hurry!

way to the beach. Once there, we headed west just like Petunia had instructed. The sand was **squishy** beneath my paws, and once or twice I felt like I may have stepped on a **SEA CRAB**. I tried not to think about it. Did I mention I'm not big on crusty sea creatures? Especially ones that like to **pinch** you with their claws when you least suspect it!

Finally, after about fifteen minutes, we saw a bright **light** coming from what appeared to be a cave.

Aunt Sweetfur told Benjamin and Bugsy to *stay put* while we went ahead to investigate. I was dying to stay put myself, but how could I send an old lady off *alone* in the **DARK**?

Slowly, we crept forward toward the light. When we reached the CAVE, we peeked inside.

Sitting around a CAMPFIRE were the Provolone children and Captain Crooked Paw. They were squeaking and LAUGHiNG like old friends. In a corner, I spotted poor Professsor Fishywhiskers tied up like a salami, and in the center of the cave sat The Eye of the Ocean.

"You'd better tell us how to open that oyster, Professor, if you know what's good for you!" Simon threatened.

But the professor refused to SQUEAK.

"Hey, Simon," Sinbad piped up, "how about we break the shell with this hammer?"

"Good idea," Simon snickered, reaching for the tool.

This sent the professor into a frenzy.

"No!" he shrieked. "That oyster is a RARE treasure! A **priceless** discovery! A UNIQUE specimen! A . . ."

Aunt Sweetfur and I tiptoed away. Maybe if the professor could keep the crooks talking, we could think of some way to help.

At that moment, Benjamin and Bugsy Wugsy ran up to us.

"Look who we found!" they cried.

THE GHOST OF SHELL ISLAND

The voice I heard in the **DARK** made my heart skip.

"Did you bring the *flute*, G?"

It was Petunia!

"Sorry I worried you," she whispered, taking the flute from me.

"What are we going to do?" I asked.

"Don't worry. I've got a **plan**. Listen carefully. . . ." Petunia began.

I grinned. I should have known Petunia would figure out what to do. Now do you see why I like her so much? That mouse thinks of **everything**!

Following Petunia, we **CLIMBED** up the rocks to the top of the cave. Petunia pointed to a small crevice on the cave's ceiling, which gave us a perfect view inside.

"Okay, it's up to you," Petunia whispered to Benjamin. "Do you **remember** what to say?"

He nodded, leaning toward the crack.

Then he took a deep breath and bellowed at the top of his lungs, "You miserable rodents! How dare you enter my sacred cave!"

As Petunia had predicted, Benjamin's voice reverberated throughout the cave like thunder. It sounded so SCARY, I had to remind myself it was just my nephew.

Meanwhile, the Provolone siblings and the captain turned as WHITE as four slices of mozzarella!

Benjamin covered his mouth to keep from LAUGHING.

"Wh-who are you?" the captain asked.

"I am the ghost of Shell Island! How dare you steal one of my most beautiful daughters from my waters?!" Benjamin yelled.

"We didn't steal it, we found it!" Simon insisted. "Besides, how do we know you're not a crook?"

"How dare you call me a crook? Now you will pay!" my nephew shouted.

At this, Petunia quickly approached the crack and began playing the flute.

"Is this a joke?" asked Simon, looking around. But just then the oyster's shell began to open, revealing its great treasure: the enormouse pearl!

That was Professor Fishywhiskers's secret. The shell would open at the sound of music!

"Let's grab it and get out of here!" cried the captain, *hurling* himself toward the pearl. The Provolone siblings followed him.

"Good-bye, pearl," I murmured.

But Petunia had a plan. She waited until those crooks stretched their

------------->

paws toward the pearl and then she suddenly stopped playing. The shell shut on their paws with a loud **snap!**

"Help! Let us go!" they cried.

"Promise you will never set paw in this cave ever again!" Benjamin yelled into the crack.

"We promise!" yelled the crooks, sobbing like baby mouselets.

Then Petunia played a few notes on the flute and the shell opened. Captain Crooked Paw and the Provolone siblings TOOK OFF with their tails between their legs.

"You think we'll ever see them again, Uncle G?" Benjamin asked.

"Not a GHOST of a chance!" I replied. And everyone laughed.

Twenty minutes later, we loaded the oyster back onto the laboratory ship.

"TO NEW MOUSE CITY!" Professor Fishywhiskers cheered as we set sail with our precious treasure safe and sound.

A GOOD LUCK CHARM

On the day they opened the new exhibit at the **New Mouse City Aquarium**, **everyone** was there: Mayor Frederick Fuzzypaws, Professor Fishywhiskers, the entire staff of *The Rodent's Gazette*, and lots of other curious rodents.Naturally, we were all there as well.

Even though I had been the one to **find** the oyster, I knew it was just dumb luck that had led me to it. I tried my best to let Petunia do all the talking. After all, if it wasn't for her **DOCUMENTARY** we would have never been on Shell Island in the first place!

But when all the photographers began

snapping photos, Petunia wanted me right by her side. Picture it, me side by side with the most fascinating rodent on all of Mouse Island, the *rodent of my dreams*! I was in heaven!

Then, just when I thought things couldn't get any more exciting, the most faBumouSe music began playing from the overhead speakers. To everyone's surprise, The Eye of the Ocean slowly opened, revealing the **enormouse** pearl inside.

"OOOOOOOOOOOOOOOOOOOOOOOOOH!"
the crowd gasped in amazement.

I took that moment to whisper to my aunt Sweetfur the one question I had been meaning to ask her.

Why did she have a *flute* in her suitcase on our trip?

"It's a special gift Uncle Grayfur gave me many years ago. It's my good luck charm! I take it with me wherever I go." She beamed. "I showed Petunia on the plane ride over to Shell Island. Isn't that LUCKY?"

I smiled. It sure was!

I gazed again at the enormouse pearl before me, and then at Petunia by my side. No, I didn't have a good luck charm like Aunt Sweetfur, but right then I felt like the luckiest rodent on Mouse Island!

Don't miss any of my other fabumouse adventures!

#1 Lost Treasure of the Emerald Eye

#2 The Curse of the Cheese Pyramid

#3 Cat and Mouse in a Haunted House

#4 I'm Too Fond of My Fur!

#5 Four Mice Deep in the Jungle

#6 Paws Off, Cheddarface!

#7 Red Pizzas for a Blue Count

#8 Attack of the Bandit Cats

#9 A Fabumouse Vacation for Geronimo

#10 All Because of a Cup of Coffee

#11 It's Halloween, You 'Fraidy Mouse!

#12 Merry Christmas, Geronimo!

#13 The Phantom of the Subway

#14 The Temple of the Ruby of Fire

#15 The Mona Mousa Code

#16 A Cheese-Colored Camper

#17 Watch Your Whiskers, Stilton!

#18 Shipwreck on the Pirate Islands

#19 My Name Is Stilton, Geronimo Stilton

#20 Surf's Up, Geronimo!

#21 The Wild, Wild West

#22 The Secret of Cacklefur Castle

A Christmas Tale

#23 Valentine's Day Disaster

#24 Field Trip to Niagara Falls

#25 The Search for Sunken Treasure

#26 The Mummy with No Name

#27 The Christmas Toy Factory

#28 Wedding Crasher

#29 Down and Out Down Under

#30 The Mouse Island Marathon

#31 The Mysterious Cheese Thief

Christmas Catastrophe

#32 Valley of the Giant Skeletons

#33 Geronimo and the Gold Medal Mystery

#34 Geronimo Stilton, Secret Agent

#35 A Very Merry Christmas

#36 Geronimo's Valentine

#37 The Race Across America

#38 A Fabumouse School Adventure

#39 Singing Sensation

#40 The Karate Mouse

#41 Mighty Mount Kilimanjaro

#42 The Peculiar Pumpkin Thief

#43 I'm Not a Supermouse!

#44 The Giant Diamond Robbery

#45 Save the White Whale!

#46 The Haunted Castle

#47 Run for the Hills, Geronimo!

#48 The Mystery in Venice

#49 The Way of the Samurai

#50 This Hotel Is Haunted

#51 The Enormouse Pearl Heist

And coming soon!

#52 Mouse in Space!

Don't miss these very special editions!

THE KINGDOM OF FANTASY

THE QUEST FOR PARADISE:
THE RETURN TO THE KINGDOM OF FANTASY

THE AMAZING VOYAGE:
THE THIRD ADVENTURE IN THE KINGDOM OF FANTASY

THE DRAGON PROPHECY:
THE FOURTH ADVENTURE IN THE KINGDOM OF FANTASY

THEA STILTON:
THE JOURNEY TO ATLANTIS

Thea Stilton's first hardcover!

Be sure to check out these exciting Thea Sisters adventures!

Thea Stilton and the Dragon's Code

Thea Stilton and the Mountain of Fire

Thea Stilton and the Ghost of the Shipwreck

Thea Stilton and the Secret City

Thea Stilton and the Mystery in Paris

Thea Stilton and the Cherry Blossom Adventure

Thea Stilton and the Star Castaways

Thea Stilton: Big Trouble in the Big Apple

Thea Stilton and the Ice Treasure

Thea Stilton and the Secret of the Old Castle

Thea Stilton and the Blue Scarab Hunt

Thea Stilton and the Prince's Emerald

Meet
CREEPELLA VON CACKLEFUR

I, *Geronimo Stilton*, have a lot of mouse friends, but none as **spooky** as my friend CREEPELLA VON CACKLEFUR! She is an enchanting and MYSTERIOUS mouse with a pet bat named **Bitewing**. YIKES! I'm a real 'fraidy mouse, but even I think CREEPELLA and her family are AWFULLY fascinating. I can't wait for you to read all about CREEPELLA in these fa-mouse-ly funny and **spectacularly spooky** tales!

#1 THE THIRTEEN GHOSTS

#2 MEET ME IN HORRORWOOD

#3 GHOST PIRATE TREASURE

#4 RETURN OF THE VAMPIRE

ABOUT THE AUTHOR

 Born in New Mouse City, Mouse Island, **GERONIMO STILTON** is Rattus Emeritus of Mousomorphic Literature and of Neo-Ratonic Comparative Philosophy. For the past twenty years, he has been running *The Rodent's Gazette*, New Mouse City's most widely read daily newspaper.

Stilton was awarded the Ratitzer Prize for his scoops on *The Curse of the Cheese Pyramid* and *The Search for Sunken Treasure*. He has also received the Andersen 2000 Prize for Personality of the Year. One of his bestsellers won the 2002 eBook Award for world's best ratlings' electronic book. His works have been published all over the globe.

In his spare time, Mr. Stilton collects antique cheese rinds and plays golf. But what he most enjoys is telling stories to his nephew Benjamin.

1. Main entrance
2. Printing presses (where the books and newspaper are printed)
3. Accounts department
4. Editorial room (where the editors, illustrators, and designers work)
5. Geronimo Stilton's office
6. Helicopter landing pad

THE RODENT'S GAZETTE

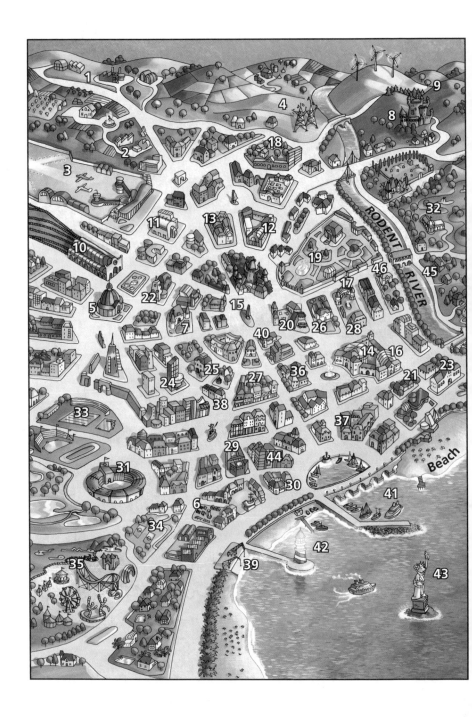

Map of New Mouse City

1. Industrial Zone
2. Cheese Factories
3. Angorat International Airport
4. WRAT Radio and Television Station
5. Cheese Market
6. Fish Market
7. Town Hall
8. Snotnose Castle
9. The Seven Hills of Mouse Island
10. Mouse Central Station
11. Trade Center
12. Movie Theater
13. Gym
14. Catnegie Hall
15. Singing Stone Plaza
16. The Gouda Theater
17. Grand Hotel
18. Mouse General Hospital
19. Botanical Gardens
20. Cheap Junk for Less (Trap's store)
21. Aunt Sweetfur and Benjamin's house
22. Mouseum of Modern Art
23. University and Library
24. *The Daily Rat*
25. *The Rodent's Gazette*
26. Trap's House
27. Fashion District
28. The Mouse House Restaurant
29. Environmental Protection Center
30. Harbor Office
31. Mousidon Square Garden
32. Golf Course
33. Swimming Pool
34. Tennis Courts
35. Curlyfur Island Amusement Park
36. Geronimo's House
37. Historic District
38. Public Library
39. Shipyard
40. Thea's House
41. New Mouse Harbor
42. Luna Lighthouse
43. The Statue of Liberty
44. Hercule Poirat's Office
45. Petunia Pretty Paws's House
46. Grandfather William's House

Brigand's Isle

This way to the Rodent Straits

Pirate Ship of Cats

Tomcat Island

Hamster Islands

Blue Dolphin Bay

Coral Reefs

This way to the Mousific Ocean

Stray Cat Harbor

San Mouscisco

Mousefort Beach

Furflung Island

This way to the Sea of Mice

Cat's Claw Bay

Panther Archipelago

Swissville

Cheddarton

Mouseport

This way to the Ratlantic Ocean

New Mouse City

2 3 4
1
6 7
5
25 8
9 14
11 13
12
10 23
32 15 21
20 22
29 19 26 17 16
18 35
27 28 30 24
31 36
33 37
34

N
W   E
S

MOUSE ISLAND

Map of Mouse Island

1. Big Ice Lake
2. Frozen Fur Peak
3. Slipperyslopes Glacier
4. Coldcreeps Peak
5. Ratzikistan
6. Transratania
7. Mount Vamp
8. Roastedrat Volcano
9. Brimstone Lake
10. Poopedcat Pass
11. Stinko Peak
12. Dark Forest
13. Vain Vampires Valley
14. Goose Bumps Gorge
15. The Shadow Line Pass
16. Penny Pincher Castle
17. Nature Reserve Park
18. Las Ratayas Marinas
19. Fossil Forest
20. Lake Lake
21. Lake Lakelake
22. Lake Lakelakelake
23. Cheddar Crag
24. Cannycat Castle
25. Valley of the Giant Sequoia
26. Cheddar Springs
27. Sulfurous Swamp
28. Old Reliable Geyser
29. Vole Vale
30. Ravingrat Ravine
31. Gnat Marshes
32. Munster Highlands
33. Mousehara Desert
34. Oasis of the Sweaty Camel
35. Cabbagehead Hill
36. Rattytrap Jungle
37. Rio Mosquito

Dear mouse friends,
Thanks for reading, and farewell
till the next book.
It'll be another whisker-licking-good
adventure, and that's a promise!

Geronimo Stilton